NORFOLK RHYMES

Edited By Kelly Scannell

First published in Great Britain in 2018 by:

Young Writers
Remus House
Coltsfoot Drive
Peterborough
PE2 9BF
Telephone: 01733 890066
Website: www.youngwriters.co.uk

All Rights Reserved
Book Design by Ben Reeves
© Copyright Contributors 2018
SB ISBN 978-1-78896-847-8
Printed and bound in the UK by BookPrintingUK
Website: www.bookprintinguk.com
YB0378U

FOREWORD

Young Writers was created in 1991 with the express purpose of promoting and encouraging creative writing. Each competition we create is tailored to the relevant age group, hopefully giving each child the inspiration and incentive to create their own piece of writing, whether it's a poem or a short story. We truly believe that seeing it in print gives pupils a sense of achievement and pride in their work and themselves.

Our latest competition, Monster Poetry, focuses on uncovering the different techniques used in poetry and encouraging pupils to explore new ways to write a poem. Using a mix of imagination, expression and poetic styles, this anthology is an impressive snapshot of the inventive, original and skilful writing of young people today. These poems showcase the creativity and talent of these budding new writers as they learn the skills of writing, and we hope you are as entertained by them as we are.

CONTENTS

Independent Entries

Amelia Sellers (9) — 1

Avenue Junior School, Norwich

Arnie Sykes (8)	2
Sammy Belderson (9)	4
Lola Kennett (9) & Evie	6
Alice Saxton (8)	8
Elizabeth Ava Moscou (8)	10
Sylvie Rowbury (8)	12
Robbie Hamilton Woodhouse (9)	14
Alex Carr (8)	16
Charles Fitzgerald (8)	18
Bryony Gaffney (10)	19
Daisy Kennett (8)	20
Hetty Harris (8)	21
Rosa Hammond (10)	22
Mia Scarlett Ottewell (8)	23
Joshua Michael Saunders (9)	24
Albie Ellis Gridley (8)	25
Grace Duarte (8)	26
Nathan Young (7)	27
Ezra Albert Gibson Anderson (8)	28
Florence Kemm (9)	29
Eli Bingley (8)	30
Hedy Denton (8)	31
Eva Tizzard Taylor (7)	32
Lola White (8)	33
Josephine Bloomfield (8)	34
Abby Soeng-Pearson (8)	35
Sophie Hattersley (8)	36
Rose Cooper McCaul (7)	37
Mia Rose Paley (8)	38
Evie Mae Fitch (9)	39
Billy Potter (8)	40
Valentina Bee Davies-Haywood (9)	41
Joe Williams (8)	42
Noonah Anari Miron-Patel (9)	43
Maryam Batool Meddings (7)	44
Isobel Lemmon (9)	45
Florence Milner-Smith (8)	46
Jenny Moore (8)	47
Mollie Colbourn (7)	48
Bella Sawyer (8)	49
Zack Archer (7)	50
Eva Hill (8)	51
Ewan Hammond (8)	52
Mason James Stephen O'Leary (9)	53
Bonny Milner (9)	54
Sarah Willis (9)	55
Ana Moschakis (8)	56
Daisy Vine (8)	57
Elliott Smith (7)	58
Evie Arianna Lee (9)	59
Ruby Pollard (10)	60
Madelyn May Walker-Collins (7)	61
Maddy Bowden (8)	62
Florence Ivy Morris (8)	63
Ayah Guenaoui (8)	64
Emma Wernham (8)	65
Faith Wierzchleyski (8)	66
Amber Rose Greengrass (8)	67
Millie Sharman (8)	68
Mabel Hutchins (7)	69
Elina Kasiri (8)	70
Rodrigo Pedroso (7)	71
Eva Frary (7)	72
Freddie Sweeting (7)	73

Biba Cropper (8)	74
Tazkiyah Anam Rahman (8)	75
Fin Taylor (7)	76
Ivan Newby (8)	77
Gregor Rogers (9)	78
Giorgio Mckenzie (8)	79
Felicity Colyer-O'Brien (7)	80
Florence Josephine Mae Warner (7)	81
Aksharaa Subashkaran (7)	82
Jacob Willgress-Quinn (8)	83
Alex Wilson (8)	84
Lily Mae Blunsten (8)	85
Jemima Kirkham (9)	86
William Shaw (8)	87
Angel (8)	88
Nikolai Brookes (9)	89
Martha Selby (9)	90
Luca Seatter-Jones (9)	91
Chloe Fleming (8)	92
Percy Manka-Taylor (8)	93
Dylann Bothma (8)	94
Ruby Hauxwell-Baldwin (9)	95
Jack Bailey (9)	96
Oscar Colyer-O'Brien (8)	97

Cromer Junior School, Cromer

Éléna Inacio (10)	98
Ava Skillen (9)	100
Molly Jayne Postle (10)	102
Daisy Goodwin (8) & Scarlett Keeler	104
Leah Louise Dawson (10)	105
Hazel Broughton (9)	106
Ivy Broughton (11)	107
Paige Matthews (9)	108
Charlotte Daniels (8)	109
Summer Marie Mclean (9)	110
Matthew Aidan Williams (11)	111
Darcy Dagless (8)	112
Issy Carey (11)	113
Megan Hawkes (11)	114
Ruby Giovannoni (8)	115
Isla Gull (8)	116

Eaton Primary School, Norwich

Rosalind Pope-Norton (10)	117
Natasha Simpkin (10)	118
Bailey Philpot (10)	120
Isla Valpied (10)	122
Ollie Williams (10)	123
Matthew Abbs (10)	124
Summer Geitner (9)	125
Isobella Lea Solomon (10)	126
Florence Bacon (8)	127
Robert Alston (10)	128
Eva Whitehead (8)	129
Olivia-Graice Overton (8)	130
Dylan Vlotman (10)	131
Cole Bryce (8)	132
Scarlet Mills (8)	133
Megan Flute (10)	134
Rudi Pearson Bray (10)	135
Honey Myers (8)	136
Guy Jackets (10)	137
Aamina Farooq (9)	138
Jack Christopher Grint (8)	139

Fairstead Community Primary & Nursery School, Fairstead

Cyprian Dron (8)	140
Ruby Feder (8)	141
Ruby Taylor-Moore (8)	142
Isabelle Akisanya (7)	143
Dylan Anthony Jack Mattinson (8)	144
Isabella Higgins (8)	145
Miley Robertson (8)	146
Zarrel Dunn (8)	147
Harvey Buonaiuto (8)	148
Laeila Buttifant (7)	149
Antoni Ostasz (7)	150
Kayleigh Buttifant (7)	151
Curtis Grimes (8)	152
Amelia Fysh (7)	153

Kristers Trecaks (8)	154
Zack Goncalves (8)	155
Sofia Grisina (8)	156
Aaron Gent (8)	157
Jayden Shuttleworth-Green (8)	158
Daisy-Louise Xanthe Gibbs (8)	159
Nikolas Kriukov (7)	160
Amaru Casaleiro (8)	161
Ryley Michael George Bull (8)	162
Ella-Louise Audrey Lewis (8)	163
Darby-Cole Mannering (8)	164
Faith Good (7)	165
Jack Bunting (8)	166
Jasmine Collison (7)	167
Mercedes Shackcloth (8)	168
Roberts Anisimovs (8)	169
Paris Curry (7)	170

Fred Nicholson School, Dereham

Hayden Cork (11)	171
Charlie Steven Marchlewicz (9)	172
Rylee Towell (11)	173
Zak Robertson (11)	174
Courtney Rebecca McDowell (13)	175
Abbey Weir (11)	176
Jacob Christian-Luck (11)	177
Maddison Malone (11)	178
Kyle Ravanera (12)	179

Mundesley Junior School, Mundesley

Bodhi Foulser (8)	180
Ella Hamilton (8)	181
Mila Carlton-Paterson (8)	182
Sophie Roberts (8)	183
Isla Grace Thomson (8)	184
Sophie Ducker (8)	185
Katelyn Freeman (8)	186
Sophie May Howard (8)	187
Courtney Wymer (7)	188
Ruby Marsden (7)	189

Evie-Mai West (8)	190
Kiera Light (8)	191
Luke Gray (7)	192
Millie Rogers (8)	193
Matthew Taylor (8)	194
Imi Whiting (7)	195
Logan Reid (8)	196
Iwan Thomas (8)	197

Sandringham & West Newton CE Primary School, West Newton

Lilly Hickling (9)	198
Pleasance Allen (8)	201
Oliver Herbert (9)	202
Elliot Wright (8)	205
Darcie Askew (8)	206
Clara Moreland (9)	208
Chloe Southwell (9)	210
Kaden Underwood (8)	212
Henry McLeish (8)	214
Sienna Fellowes (9)	217
George Wood (8)	218
Evelyn Wright-Thompson (8)	220
Ella Southwell (9)	222
Caitlin Jayne Ward (8)	224
Daisy May (8)	226
Elizabeth Wright (8)	228
Elliott Harrod (8)	230

THE POEMS

The Horrorficator

Beware,
She's coming, venomous fangs, magical powers, evil eyes
She hunts for power, she haunts your bedroom, be afraid
Her blood-dripping fangs under your bed
Beware,
She lurks in your house, waiting... waiting for her next victim to come
Beware,
She's near, somewhere here, she's coming
I'm warning you, run or else
Beware,
She's come, you're dead, I told you don't get in bed!
Beware,
It's the Horrorficator, could you be next?
Beware.

Amelia Sellers (9)

The Gobbernorf!

G obbernorf, a ferocious, mechanical blob of magma with a tongue of boiling coal

O n the 25th of every month, this monster comes to torment, he takes each and every little child out of their cosy beds,

B ut one of the children tried to escape and, remarkably, they succeeded, the child was running away with the Gobbernorf on his tail, he ran past a convenience store and saw the Daily Mail,

'B oris Johnson lost his pants in a scene of grasshoppers hopping' was the headline of the bemusing article

E very step of the Gobbernorf was a boom of despicable thunder, getting closer and closer, then all of a sudden...

R oarrrrrr! bellowed the monster, releasing hundreds of drops of saliva from its jaws

N efariously, monstrously, deviously, the Gobbernorf leapt into the air with great force and power, then landed

O n top of a shower! The Gobbernorf was bewildered to see his mother, who was extremely sour, he

R an away as fast as the speed of light, hoping to never see her again!
F inally, we get to the end of this wondrous poem (just being modest), hope you enjoyed it, bye!

Arnie Sykes (8)
Avenue Junior School, Norwich

The Wobble Duck Cream

The Wobble Duck Cream was a killer of humans, it had a poisonous bite
And the humans would plummet to the floor
Its body and head were the shape of a duck but it was covered in cream
And it wobbled in an odd manner
It was from the planet Jupiter, and it loved to eat humans
It travelled back and forth between Jupiter and Earth
In a spaceship on Jupiter, he had built a huge gun
Covered in beaky cream, it took eight and a half years to build and
Finally, he got the last part for it
His plan was to destroy Mercury because
His arch-enemy lived there
The Wobble Duck Cream was so excited
He didn't notice a Mercury spy ship land
The Wobble Duck Cream put the last part of the gun into the gun
It started to work, he aimed at Mercury

But just when it was going to fire, a few Mercury spies
Jumped out and headbutted the gun, it rotated and
Hit Earth instead, *boom!* Earth blew up,
The Wobble Duck Cream said, "Oi, that's my dinner!"

Sammy Belderson (9)
Avenue Junior School, Norwich

An Adventure Awaits!

An adventure awaits!
As I walk into the dark forest,
Lonely, sad and forlorn as a monster should be
The sky disappeared overhead,
As it did, I dropped my head
Suddenly, the rain fell
As I tiptoed through the grassy moor,
Out of the corner of my eye
A shelter I saw, I ran inside to get away
From a dreadful thought of another day.
In the cave, at once I saw,
A pretty picture on the wall.
Inspired by the drawing, my heart started to flutter,
I found a chalk, I found a wall
And all at once, I started to draw
Happily, I coloured all night, all day
'Til the day came to an end.
Amazed by this incredible sight,
All I wanted to do was take flight

Some more joyful monsters I saw,
Colourful, creative and more,
I was as happy as a balloon about to burst
I had finally made friends.
That's the end of my story,
But 'm sure a new one is soon to begin.

Lola Kennett (9) & Evie
Avenue Junior School, Norwich

Magpie And Me!

There was a fiery, flickering, flaming volcano
That was over 2,000 metres!
There lived Magpie now,
The thing about Magpie was
It was badder than anything you can imagine!
Magpie is red, brave and fluffy
Its wings shine and shimmer in the moonlight
Flames burn off its wings that hide the stars,
Its talons like lightning shooting from its claws.

Now, at the weekend, I sneak slowly through my flat
Down the crooked stairs and out the door,
The way to the mountain keeps me counting my steps!
Downhill all the way
It's boiling when I climb up the treacherous volcano.

We're always up to no good
Stealing from sales of sweetie shops
We ate them all! The lot!

People think we're imbeciles because we steal,
But they're the imbeciles because they call the cops!
It's only sugary sweets that pop!

So, we have lots and lots of fun, fun, fun!

Alice Saxton (8)
Avenue Junior School, Norwich

The Purple Blob

My blob was born in a volcano and rose to the surface
To make the world a happy place and stop evil
When it jumps, it kills evil
It has eyes as green as the sun
It's tiny but magical, nothing can kill it
Because it is made out of jelly
So a sword just gets stuck.
It's best friends with Little Rainbow Blob
And they go to parties together and play together
And have lots of enjoyment!
Jumping skills means it can always win the long jump
It likes to go to the Olympics and makes lots of friends
And it can shoot heart balls from its tail
It never takes off its party hat,
It doesn't like the beach
Because if the golden sand gets on it,
It will stick and never come off.

It lives on Blob Island
It smells like grapes, freshly picked from the tree
As green as a leaf,
It eats biscuits then it vanishes and never comes back!

Elizabeth Ava Moscou (8)
Avenue Junior School, Norwich

What's Your Name?

My monster came alive on Saturn
And went on a rocket to Earth
He found himself in a field, my dad's field
It was on a hill, he fell down and down
And round and round and he forgot
His name, which I did not know
When I saw him, he had as many eyes as an alien
Wait a minute, he was an alien
He was as colourful as a rainbow
He was really long, he was really frilly
He told me about lots of things
About how he had two friends, one was called Spike
And one was called Candyfloss, he said they were nice
We went to the beach, and ate all the ice cream
From an ice cream van
And we went to the zoo and saw some animals
He thought some of the animals looked like him
But they were pandas

He got a spaceship back to Saturn
And we never even knew each other's names.

Sylvie Rowbury (8)
Avenue Junior School, Norwich

Orochi And Bloodlust

One day in the hell factory
The Blood Luster awoke, not abruptly
He said, from the deep bloodbath,
"Orochi, your time is over
Now I'm out."
You can't win
Over on Earth
In Dover
Two humans teleport to hell
World factory
They see Blood Luster, they scream
They run until they reach a throne
Which opens where Orochi sits
"He's out, I feel it," he says
They ask Orochi for help
He gets up and says
"Blood Luster, I'm back again."
They fight day and night
Orochi gets hit down
In one human's pocket

There's a sonic wave translator
He says to it, "Please Mumsy."
He says, "Okay, my son."
They are there in Dover
Phew, it's over!

Robbie Hamilton Woodhouse (9)
Avenue Junior School, Norwich

Sun And The War

In a deep, dark, deadly house,
There was a deadly monster.
His name was Sun,
He was a deadly shadow monster
Everyone was nice to Sun
So Sun was nice to them
He played with the children
One day, a huge war broke out
So Sun had to keep the children safe
So he got all of the children to their mums and dads.
Then he flew away himself
With his camouflaged wings
He settled himself on the top of a tree
But some baddies were there
So he flew away to a strange island
When the war ended, he flew back
But no one was there
So he flew over the border
For many days and nights he flew
Finally, he found them in New Zealand

So he made a new home
People were glad to see him
Everyone was happy.

Alex Carr (8)
Avenue Junior School, Norwich

Slagerbob's Big Adventure

Hey, have you heard of Slagerbob?
No, thought not, well this is the story of him
At 7:34am and 37 seconds, on a Saturday,
He was born with his sister,
By the way, they're twins
And that's the start of a hard life
Ten years later, it was breakfast time in the household
Crunch! Chew! Chew! Crunch!
Ooo, la la, this is delicious,
Then his sister went out for a stroll
Then she was shot in the head by a ninja
Well not shot in the head
Hit in the head by a ninja throwing star
Slagerbob was outraged so...
Three years later, he had successfully built a nuke
Set the nuke off, ran to his secret bunker
The nuke blew up and killed everyone in the world.

Charles Fitzgerald (8)
Avenue Junior School, Norwich

Lights Out

Darkness covered my entire bedroom, like a suffocating blanket,
a glint of menace in his bloodshot eyes.
As he passed, it seemed as if all the happiness had been sucked out of the world.

I could see his long bony fingers reaching out for me as if
I was a fly in a spider's web.
His cloak making unsettling shadows all around the room.
Anything could crawl out from the cave that was my wardrobe.

Darkness was silent, though in my head, it felt like one million
screams were piercing my ears.
It was as if I was in the presence of death himself.

I woke up in the morning.
Only another twelve hours until the monster visited me again...

Bryony Gaffney (10)
Avenue Junior School, Norwich

The Friend

Fluff lived on the gigantic, death-defying moon
That sparkled like sequins in the night
Fluff was as soft as a cushion
Fluff's ears were as velvety as a silk carpet
One day, Fluff left the moon when the stars shone
And travelled for an end until Fluff was exhausted
Fluff got to England without knowing
Fluff tried to find a place to stay but Fluff didn't find anywhere
Suddenly, out of nowhere, a little monster came up
And offered a place to stay, it was beautiful and peaceful
So Fluff took the offer and they became best friends forever
They rode horses together, they baked together
They basically did everything together.

Daisy Kennett (8)
Avenue Junior School, Norwich

All In France

I found a little man in a can
It had one eye and teeth like blades
We sat down on a bench
My monster was French
It had ten maids
We played I Spy
I spotted a cat with my eye
The cat got angry and planned to attack
The monster dodged, how the cat sobbed
It nearly died and then it flew,
Because the cat flicked it onto a mat
I just found out its name was Nob,
I really wanted to call it Bob
Its weakness is gobstoppers, they're Nob-stoppers
The sky went purple when Nob saw a turtle
The turtle could fly
It made some pie
The pie was nice, nearly as nice as rice
Nob lived happily so did the turtle.

Hetty Harris (8)
Avenue Junior School, Norwich

Roar

Miss, why is Griffin so short?
Miss, why does Griffin have horns?
Miss, why is Griffin so hairy?
Miss, why is Griffin a... monster?
Nerdy, geeky, loves to read
Lives on mountains, climbs up trees
Swims in rivers, pees in the reeds
Shy, wary, alert
The best at maths, the best at reading
But his grammar is awfully shocking
Flowers dancing in the breeze
He joins in grinning with glee
But Griffin gets bullied, picked on,
Teased, spat on, Griffin hides in the trees
Swaying in the breeze
The bullies find him
The bullies shout at him
But who's the best at shouting?
Griffin is... *Roar!*

Rosa Hammond (10)
Avenue Junior School, Norwich

Cute Monster, Ugly Monster

In a deep, dark cave, full of glass-shattering shrieks
I found a cute monster with two hairy ears and six sharp teeth
We talked and had some fun before the real adventure began
Its name was Fang and her and I became friends in no time
We looked at the back of the cave and saw a black hole in mid-daylight
We travelled through, out the cave until…
Suddenly, out of nowhere, a huge growl, as large as a bear
Out crawled a big, hairy monster
We tried to run but our legs would not move
Shaking in fear, we finally moved and ran and ran
Until I fell but when I stood up,
Everything had disappeared
Was it true or was it fake?

Mia Scarlett Ottewell (8)
Avenue Junior School, Norwich

The Monster

He's neither your friend nor your foe,
Because his heart's full of sadness and woe
His mother, an old hag, one day packed her gone for good bag
Now all by himself, in the candlestick tree,
Darkness is all he can see
He feels sad and alone
And shattered to the bone
What shall be done, where shall he go?
Should he ride on the back of a black, black crow?
Then suddenly, *bang*, in the darkest of nights,
Dazzling bright lights, what a sight
No, he will find himself a dove,
That way he's sure to have love
He's not a foe but a friend,
And that's how his poem will end.

Joshua Michael Saunders (9)
Avenue Junior School, Norwich

The Big Bad Monster

A monster invaded my town and he made a home
In a deep, deep, dark cave, it had
He had two devils that were as red as blood
He had horns as big as an arm
And his fangs were razor-sharp teeth
And as hairy as a woolly mammoth
His eyes were as black as night
His claws were as white as clouds
His spots were as big as a car wheel
I was going on a hike
I heard the monster's roar
And I quickly dug a pit
And I put it near his cave
Then some people came and
When they just got there
The monster fell in the pit and
The people cheered and I smiled
My teeth glistened in the sun...

Albie Ellis Gridley (8)
Avenue Junior School, Norwich

Riding Tomorrow

Once at the end of a rainbow
There lived a tiny monster the size of a flower.
It was cute and as cuddly as a toy
Its favourite thing to eat was strawberries and cotton candy
It was only three at the time and it was being extremely naughty
Because it slid down the rainbow
And if you kept walking, you would eventually come
To the exit of Imagination Land.
So it kept walking until it was in the human world
Soon, it came across a girl and she was walking along the street,
She was going to the pet shop when the monster popped out
She took him home and she went to his house
And they lived happily!

Grace Duarte (8)
Avenue Junior School, Norwich

Day Of The Devil

Smelldon, the monster, was born
in Poopsilla
He loved chaos
He found a fly, in the dark sky
But it was always dark because
He was all so big
And black
The fly said hi
And then bye
But before bye,
"How about a picnic?"
"Yes, sure," Smelldon said.
But the fly thought he would lie
But no, even Smelldon thought so.
This time he decided to glow
Although he was dark as a black mark
He crept up on the fly
So he didn't light up the dark sky
He crunched the fly
So again, no light, no light, no light,
He couldn't help crunching.

Nathan Young (7)
Avenue Junior School, Norwich

Long Tongue's Sad Poem

Long Tongue was scruffy but smart,
He held a pocket watch in his hand
I met him in a castle
The name of it was Warwick Castle
You see I never knew a monster
Would be lying in his nest at a castle
Oh, I forgot to tell you about his tongue
It was long, very long, as long as a frog's
Anyway, one day, we went to Norwich Castle
We went to Cromer as well
Went to the shops for an hour and a day
And we played at the beach
And ate lots of peach
After one more day, we went back home
And went to bed.
In the morning I looked at the end of my bed
And the monster was gone.

Ezra Albert Gibson Anderson (8)
Avenue Junior School, Norwich

The Squoogle Worm

Killer of all creatures
Long, twinderly tail, slicing and slithering around
Watery creatures' necks.

One measly eye, slipping, sitting in its too big socket
Writhing, wriggling against the tide.

The sparkling stars turn inky back
When the Squoogle worm is around.

So strong suckers groping blindly in the murk
Until it finds what it is looking for
Two mouths sucking up everything in its path.

Its wormy body writhing restlessly
Beware, the Squoogle worm is on the prowl
Lock your windows, shut your doors
It's coming, the Squoogle worm!

Florence Kemm (9)
Avenue Junior School, Norwich

A Death Chase Of A Sea Monster

I found it at last
No one dared to set it free
I had to slither out of the sea
But at last, I set it free
Will the world be angry with me?
It was blue as the sky
Lighter than the sea
For the sea monster,
I thought of a name,
Gamadose, for the blame
Will it follow me or terrorise thee?
Just get me out of here
But at last, I landed
Back in Germany but it's still after me
I'm on the run, oh no!
I've got to go, it was killed by Phill
I'm saved, thank you
Does it have a brother or sister?
But I don't mind, I'm not blind.

Eli Bingley (8)
Avenue Junior School, Norwich

Five-Eyes Hairy

Five-Eyes Hairy isn't remotely scary
He's a clumsy cuddle, a lively laugh
Five-eyed fun, the perfect friend for someone
He comes from a forest near nowhere but close to everything
With Poppy Uptown from downstairs,
Together, they travelled to space together
Their imagination grew and so did Poppy too!
Her eyes began to multiply and she didn't want to leave
The result she could not believe!
She was fluffy and horned with an orange face and paws!
A human face unlike yours,
She was an exact replica of Five-Eyes Hairy
Who isn't remotely scary.

Hedy Denton (8)
Avenue Junior School, Norwich

Mrs Big Fangs And Superman

The monster trudged by the sea
Its eyes glowing in the night
Everyone was terrified
By this horrible sight
Her horns each as big as a volcano
Mrs Big Fangs' skin was as yellow as the sun
While her fangs were dripping with blood.
And one day, she came up to me
And I ran for my life
And when I looked above me
I saw Superman with a knife
I got my net ready to catch the beast
But all she really wanted was to have a feast
She took me and Superman
On her hand and took us to her home
Again,
Where we began,
We had chocolate cake.

Eva Tizzard Taylor (7)
Avenue Junior School, Norwich

Pusheen

The fuzzy creature was born in the everlasting, never-melting Chocolate Land
It was multicoloured and it had golden, gleaming eyes
It smelt like sweet, melty chocolate
It had a rainbow tongue that tingled when she had some fun
The monster's name was Pusheen, she had a unicorn horn
And her fur was as fluffy as candyfloss
We liked to go to the funfair
We'd eat all the sweet treats and go on all the rides
Then when it was time for bed, I'd tuck her in her chocolate bed
Then we'd dream about our next adventure
And all the fun we'd have!

Lola White (8)
Avenue Junior School, Norwich

Unicandy

U nicorn and candy is what she is, lovely and caring for me and you
N ot very cruel, not at all, she will sing a lullaby for me
I n a hospital, you will see her in a lovely room, looking after some children,
C uddly and soft for nice cuddles for everyone
A t a nice cottage in Candyland is where you will seek her hiding spot
N ice and kind for you and me is how she will be,
D o you want to meet her? Yes, yes, yes she will greet you very well,
Y ou will love her, she will love you, having a nice time with her and you.

Josephine Bloomfield (8)
Avenue Junior School, Norwich

The Tiny Monster And Me

He came from ancient Africa
Waiting for an adventure
He is as green as a sunny day
He was a tiny, soft friend for you
He likes adventures
To the wild
One day, he went to the forest
And that's when he met me
He was scared of me
And I said don't be scared. He went to his house
And I said come on,
He liked to swim and that's where we went
And then that's when we
Became friends
Then he went to sea but he came back
You see, now we play every day
Though he is way smaller than me
His name is Bingerlybox.

Abby Soeng-Pearson (8)
Avenue Junior School, Norwich

Gobble

Gobble looks like candyfloss
She is soft and kind
She hugs a lot and cooks in a pot
That smells of meatball pie.
She flies through the sky
With her big blue wings
Not caring about a thing
And in the night
You glimpse the sight
Of a twinkling star above.

She was born on Mars
The pretty thing and
Is used to the heat, so
In the winter,
Her limbs will shiver
And she'll knit a blanket for warmth.
Oh, I love my Gobble
I hope you do
But just remember that every fellow
Is not as scary as you think.

Sophie Hattersley (8)
Avenue Junior School, Norwich

Fluffy

Once, I was in my garden
When I saw something moving in my bush
I looked inside and it was a green, fluffy monster!
But not all monsters are bad
He was a good one, he was my friend
He was fluffy, he was a little monster
His name was Fluffy and so we went to the park
And he told me everything
He told me that monsters didn't have mums or dads
So he was fine, he was from a monster jungle
And we were playing in the park for ages
His favourite was the swing in the park
And every morning, we went to the park and played on the swing.

Rose Cooper McCaul (7)
Avenue Junior School, Norwich

The Heart

Dark as night, creeping silently,
Huge, red devil wings
Shadow, large and domineering on this Christmas Eve,
Its old owner this small cat wants,
But it will never be,
For Kitty needs a present under the Christmas tree,
Creeping past the dark-hearted cat,
To the towering, sparkling tree,
I pull out some wool from the old, dusty sewing box,
And wrapped it to go under the tree,
To give the cat its heart back,
To give the devil its heart back,
To give the angel its heart back,
To give my guardian angel its heart back!

Mia Rose Paley (8)
Avenue Junior School, Norwich

Bob The Monster Who Always Said Boo!

B uncy Bob is a bouncy creature, he's naughty, cheeky and very noisy. Funny trickster always creeping up on you, everyone will say boo, never gets scared, always saying boo!

O h! Forgot the exciting part, he always steals from his brothers, sisters and really wants to see a human, hopes he will have a best friend.

B ob said boo, I love to say boo! I can't stop saying boo! So just stop saying it but I can't, so just boo! Bob couldn't say boo and we put Sellotape on his mouth and flushed his favourite word down the loo!

Evie Mae Fitch (9)
Avenue Junior School, Norwich

The Defence Of Planet Slime

Blooby Looby the Slimeball came from Planet Slime
He's gooey, slimy, with blue teeth, a big mouth and he's stupid
But one day, they all got attacked by Blooble Gum
They had bubblegum guns
The common name is candyfloss.
But just something funny to tell you
Candyfloss shot the king because
He was a gumball and started to do the floss
She struck one quarter of the army
So just another thing
They all ran off to Planet Earth
And when I found Blooby Looby
He ate all the cookies and cake.

Billy Potter (8)
Avenue Junior School, Norwich

Myshflumper Going

Long, long ago,
I had a monster with a bow
That one day she found me,
She was crying because she got stung by a bee.

So we went to the beach to make her feel better,
But then she got a letter
It was a letter about going,
Because she had to do lawn mowing.

So she was about to go with a person called Mo,
But then she lost her bow,
But the selfish person I am, I kept the bow,
It was time for me to go for a long time and in that long time...
I will play with some slime!

Valentina Bee Davies-Haywood (9)
Avenue Junior School, Norwich

The Scary Monster

In a deep, dark, horrifying forest
I was walking nicely when I saw a giant griffin,
a scary monster
He was staring at me like he wanted to kill me
So I ran as fast as lightning
Then my heart got really fast like a fast jaguar
It got slower and slower
Then suddenly there it was
It was staring at my face
It smelt like rotten cheese
It was as hairy as a mammoth
It had about 832 eyes!
Then a woodcutter cut down a tree
And the tree fell on the monster
Then it was destroyed.

Joe Williams (8)
Avenue Junior School, Norwich

Danger By The Sea

One day, I was walking by the beach,
And the ice cream man was there!
I went and walked up to get an ice cream,
He gave me a flavour of pistachio and pear.

Then suddenly, I heard a noise
Plop! What was that?
Did somebody drop a toy?
No, it looked something like a rainbow cat.

When I went to the water, I held the strange thing up,
Well, what was it?
It could fit in a cup!
It looked so scared and nervous that it bit its lip...

It was a monster...

Noonah Anari Miron-Patel (9)
Avenue Junior School, Norwich

The Big Friendly Monster

In a deep, dark, deadly forest,
There lived a nice, friendly, cute monster
named Gary
Gary is my friend,
He has a nice, clean, tidy cave
I met Gary in the forest
When I was having a nice walk
I hurt my foot and Gary helped me
Then I said, "Thank you."
Then he said, "You're welcome
But please do not tell anyone about me
Just keep it a secret between me and you."
We always met to play together and
We always met near the tallest tree in the forest.

Maryam Batool Meddings (7)
Avenue Junior School, Norwich

The Mer Family

There's Merzing,
And Merpal,
And Mersia too,
The sister is Merka
And yes, there's a few
They're stinky, they're slimy
They're gentle as well
If you're to see them,
You might get a smell,
They live on the planet
That's gobbledy goop
And they live on the terrible
Green sprout soup!
If you're ever to meet the Mer family
You're in for a big surprise,
If you then become friends with them,
Your happiness will just rise.

Isobel Lemmon (9)
Avenue Junior School, Norwich

Dave Mralis

Dave Mralis
Was born in McTalise.
His claws were as fluffy as a cotton tail
And he was a cat.
Dave loved to catch mice.
Dave found a mouse but he was too
Scared to catch.
Dave was a tabby cat
With green eyes like fresh cut grass.

Dave loved to roll around in the grass
When no one was lookin'.
But one day, his owner found him
Rolling around in the grass.
So he went inside and slept all day
Until tea was ready.
Then he went back to sleep.

Florence Milner-Smith (8)
Avenue Junior School, Norwich

Friends

Dave was born in a cave
Dave's skin was bright blue
With giant wings sticking out
His legs were small and floppy
Dave was kicking a stone
When he found a monster lying on the sand
"I am Leegonee Addoe," the monster said
We had some chicken meat
When Scary joined the team
We fought a monster called Rexino
We kept on fighting
"That's what friends are for,
To help each other, let's do this!" I said
We will always be friends.

Jenny Moore (8)
Avenue Junior School, Norwich

Nobble And Me

Nobble comes from the moon
He has green, shimmering skin
And lots of eyes as big as the moon
If you're being naughty,
He will come and tickle you
But one day, when he was at home
A rocket came crashing down
And hit the moon and out I came
I saw Nobble and grabbed my space gun
But then I saw the kindness in his heart
We became friends
So if you see somebody being naughty
Just run to me because I have
The Nobble in my pocket
Hee, hee, hee...

Mollie Colbourn (7)
Avenue Junior School, Norwich

The Monster In My Shoe

One day, I found a monster in my shoe,
And then he gave me quite the flu,
When I was better,
We played in the park,
Until it was midnight,
And it was dark,
He is green like silky grass,
And sometimes he is heavy like brass,
His name is Dave and he is smart,
But he hasn't a friend in his heart,
So I decided to get him a friend,
And you can guess what happened in the end
Dave was famous!
On TV
And we stayed friends for as long as can be.

Bella Sawyer (8)
Avenue Junior School, Norwich

Gligzoo The Monster

In the forest, there was a monster called Gligzoo
He found a cave and went inside
But there was a locked door.
He turned to slime and went under the door
And saw an evil cyborg crab which was giant
He turned to slime again
And the cyborg crab said, "Huh, where'd he go?"
He walked back, then Gligzoo went out
But then... he found a portal
We went in and saw a gigantic monster who was evil,
He got a giant sword and killed him and went out.

Zack Archer (7)
Avenue Junior School, Norwich

The Giant Soft Thing At The Park

One day, I found a giant soft thing in the park
With orange skin, it had a big belt on
I cuddled him, he was so silly
I was laughing
I said to him, "Do you have friends?"
He said yes, he also said he was from France
"Why do you have that belt on?" I said
He said, "My belt is for being good
If I take it off, I will be bad."
"Oh," I said, "I have hardly got teeth."
So I took him to the woods to explore.

Eva Hill (8)
Avenue Junior School, Norwich

Gooey Stomper

G lup is where I live
O n Glup, we drink loud
O nly I'm considered handsome
E aster is my birthday
Y ears are only five days long.

S wimming through the swamps, I wait for my prey to dive in
T actics are my speciality
O ranges are my only predators
M agic is my weakness
P eacemakers are a disgust to me
E asier to finally kill humans
R acers are my favourite food.

Ewan Hammond (8)
Avenue Junior School, Norwich

The Nightmare

The nightmare eating
The souls from a grave
It turns into a ball
Waits for its victim
Then it emerges into its real form
Taking the soul
Then it repeats.

The nightmare eating
The souls from a grave is repeating its pattern,
It turns from its ball into its real form
Emerging from darkness to take my soul.
Before it does I must awake
To be brave and strong for my soul not to take.
For I am not a victim of dreams I'm awake!

Mason James Stephen O'Leary (9)
Avenue Junior School, Norwich

Vicious Veilöus Shloper

Veilöus Shloper
Is a devilish soul
Sneaking in the dead of night
Catching cheeky children
Or good children for that matter.

It lives in a small town in Germany
Called Stalaley
Not many people live there
Yum yum! Children
Thought the Veilöus Shloper
His German name is obviously Veilöus Shloper
But his English name is Moonlight Man.

Don't try to fool him
You will only get
Eaten!

Bonny Milner (9)
Avenue Junior School, Norwich

Squiggle Alien

Squiggle Alien was a monster,
but he was a good monster and nobody knew it.
They called him
Moody Monster.
As slimy as a slug,
As bright as light,
As stinky as a skunk,
As weird as a beaver.
They also whispered to each other,
His behaviour is as bad as a mosquito,
His breath is as stinky as a skunk.
But one day, they found out he wasn't
as bad as they thought,
and they were friendly friends.

Sarah Willis (9)
Avenue Junior School, Norwich

Pixy Potato

There lives a girl who likes to eat
The food she likes to eat is potatoes
She ate so much, she turned into one
Now she has a little hat and
Also has a little cat
Now she saves little parks near and far
Looking after little children
She wears a cape made out of curtains
And saves many persons.
If you look up in the sky
You will see something which looks like slime
PS If you do, tell me or I'll get you.

Ana Moschakis (8)
Avenue Junior School, Norwich

Spook

Spook was born in a forest
He was sludgy and slimy
It's sometimes fluffy and soft
It can sometimes be all wet and soggy
He has a little crown
He's a little fat
It said to me, "Hello, I'm a monster."
We sat on a bench in the park
I took it home with me
I named it Spook and I kept it as my pet
I fed him lots and lots
I had to carry Spook home
He was able to fit in my palm.

Daisy Vine (8)
Avenue Junior School, Norwich

Alien Association

The Crieberced was born on Mars in the Alien Association
The Crieberced was as cold as snow
With a mouth on his tummy and
Dark, dark blue wings and two massive antennae
When he grew up, he was sent on a mission to Australia
While he lived in Australia, he found a cold cave
And that's when I met him
I promised to help with the mission
That was to blow up the world
With a massive TNT, *kaboom!*

Elliott Smith (7)
Avenue Junior School, Norwich

Boinglummer

My Boinglummer is a suck thumber
He's a lick lummer 'cause he's a boinglummer
It's fluffy and creamy pink, it's millascopic
Its Latin name is Valenpocic Cute Eyes
Eats Mute pies and not slimy, not green
Never leaves a space between small, non-scary fangs
Its signal is when a door bangs beautiful blush
And a Boinglummer is not a thumb crusher
'Cause it's only millascopic.

Evie Arianna Lee (9)
Avenue Junior School, Norwich

Finding A Friend

I found her in a jury tree
Buzzing like a bee
All alone with no friends
Until now, now I'll have a friendly mind
Though it had terrible jaws
Soft and tangled paws,
Wings all scratched,
Eye glowing like eggs just hatched
I held out my hand
Music in my heart like a band
Waiting for an answer
Like a joyful dancer
She held out her paw
Once more
Finding a friend.

Ruby Pollard (10)
Avenue Junior School, Norwich

The Tiny Fluffball!

Clay was born in Wilky Way
He had teeth as sharp as your grandma's knitting needles,
He flew over buildings with style
Arghhhh! It's a bird, it's a plane, no it's a tiny fluffball!!
Oh no! he will crash in to the bus!!
His body was covered in green fur
He was going to eat us all!
He glowed dark green,
He was about to explode! *Bang!*
A gush of wind flew past us.

Madelyn May Walker-Collins (7)
Avenue Junior School, Norwich

Pugafly

Pugafly was born on Jupiter
It has horns as purple as purple seaweed
It has scaly skin like a bearded dragon
It has an ugly face like a hippo
It has colourful eyes like a rainbow
His tail is turquoise like the ocean
Its teeth are as sharp as blades
It likes chaos
It left Jupiter on an adventure
It met me on the moon and we went to Mars
Because of the heat, he exploded.

Maddy Bowden (8)
Avenue Junior School, Norwich

Coco Monster

Coco the Monster,
Cheeky and sneaky,
Furry and cute
He was born in the jungle
With his mum and dad
But they chucked him away
And he ended up here
With the shiny blue wings
and I met him
We went together to a secret land
It had a zoo and after the zoo
We went to a shop and
He found his mum and dad
And they zoomed away
And I never saw him again.

Florence Ivy Morris (8)
Avenue Junior School, Norwich

The Horrifying Monster

In a dark, deep, horrifying forest
There lived a stupid, ugly monster
The ugly monster had ten, glowing, red lasers in her eyes
The horrifying monster had some horrifying, wimpy servants
One day, a woman who lived in a little village,
Was putting up the washing line there
When paws and hairy, ugly feet appeared,
Without hands, or a head or a body,
Suddenly... arghhhhhh!

Ayah Guenaoui (8)
Avenue Junior School, Norwich

The Evil Side

Comes from the deepest, darkest bog in the Netherlands
No one knows how long they've been there
Stares up into the fog
Eyes wandering all over the place,
Some people believe they're magical pixies,
No
They do the opposite,
Causing chaos, vicious,
Now only one of them,
It makes a great escape,
To come for you,
To come for you, Ottoline.

Emma Wernham (8)
Avenue Junior School, Norwich

Spotty

I have a pet monster called Spotty
She really is delightful and dotty
She likes to crush beetles, just for fun
But I tell her, "Oh no, not another one."
I take her to the pet shop for a treat
But everything I showed her she wouldn't eat
"No, thank you," she said, "they're full of germs,
What I like best is insects and worms."

Faith Wierzchleyski (8)
Avenue Junior School, Norwich

Rainbow Magic

My monster, my monster is called Auora
Her rainbow magic is glorious I tell you,
She is sweet and fluffy and very very cuddly
She has a baby girl, who loves to wrap up in her warm fluffy blanket
Her eyes are as blue as the ocean and her fur is as bright as a rainbow.
She's wonderful to have as my pet.
Auora is so fun and fluffy and I love her so very, very much.

Amber Rose Greengrass (8)
Avenue Junior School, Norwich

The Attack On Planet Slime

Candyfloss was born in Candy Land
He is mainly made of candyfloss
But he had candy cane antennae
And chocolate wings and Haribo teeth
One day, he teleported away from Candy Land
And to Planet Earth and met me in gravity
But back on Candy Land, Candyfloss' mother
Got so worried about him that they attacked Planet Slime
And they are still fighting today.

Millie Sharman (8)
Avenue Junior School, Norwich

My Friend

I had a friend who was cute and fluffy and had glowing red eyes
It had a very brown body and had a nice brownie smell
It lived far away in a brownie land
His little baby bot melted like a brownie chocolate
They wanted to go to Brownie Island and have some fun
But when the baby cried and died, he couldn't handle it
So he was so angry and he laid down and drooled.

Mabel Hutchins (7)
Avenue Junior School, Norwich

Enchanting Forest

In an enchanting forest, there lived an enchanting monster
Stood gleaming, out in the outstanding forest
There lived a monster called Rainbow Ice Cream
It was made out of sweets, it was as sweet as sugar
One fateful day, a falcon monster attacked
Rainbow Ice Cream saved her enchanting forest
But Falcon Monster was too strong
But Rainbow Ice Cream defeated him.

Elina Kasiri (8)
Avenue Junior School, Norwich

Zapping Earth

Fluffton was born on a star
And one day, he came down to Earth
Like a shooting star.
And the Earth shook
When he touched the Earth
It shook like an earthquake.
He had one eye and thirteen legs
And liked to cause chaos
He can shoot laser beams out of his eye.
And then he got trapped and he shot out
Then he shot his foot and got back to his star.

Rodrigo Pedroso (7)
Avenue Junior School, Norwich

Chunky's Life In Monsterland

Chunky was born in a pit
His brother is called Kit
His lava-orange tail
Is tangled on a rail
A green upper half
Yellow is his calf
One day, he left
And all the rest
Like a happy ball
Walking or crawling
I met him full of sadness,
For he had no friends
None at all,
So we made a friendship
And he was no longer alone.

Eva Frary (7)
Avenue Junior School, Norwich

Jeoff's Story

Jeoff came from a Norwich football kit
He had spiky horns, six eyes
Liked to stick his tongue out and be mischievous
And once, he even licked me
He was in-between low and high, large and thin
He was scary and cute, in-between everything
Basically, I was his best friend
We did everything together
But then something happened to him...

Freddie Sweeting (7)
Avenue Junior School, Norwich

I Met A Monster

Once I met a monster,
I met him on the sand,
He was thin and rubbery like a rubber band.
Who he was, I did not know,
It turned to winter
We played in the snow.
When it was summer, we said hello
And had a go on a pogo stick.
Then we felt sick!
I worked out his name was Fudge,
So I gave him a great big nudge.

Biba Cropper (8)
Avenue Junior School, Norwich

Spotty

Upon the moon lived a monster named Spotty.
She was rather cruel and played tricks on her friends.
She was a liar, a cheat and a thief.
Her friends said, "You are hurting our feelings."
Spotty began to wonder, *should I be kinder and less mean?*
Maybe I should be kind then they will be my friends.

Tazkiyah Anam Rahman (8)
Avenue Junior School, Norwich

Fluffy

Fluffy came from a forest
He is very fluffy, cute
He is green and he
Holds a teddy in his hand
He is good
I found him on the beach
And he was hungry
So I gave him some food
The people said, "He is bad."
I did not believe them
And they did not believe me
So Fluffy and I made friends.

Fin Taylor (7)
Avenue Junior School, Norwich

The Sainsbury's Monster

The Sainsbury Centre owned art
A monster lived behind the paintings
It was bright in colour
But the hair was sparkling purple
Purple, purple, the hair was sparkling purple.

When we met in the Sainsbury Centre
We went to Aylsham for a day
But then the day was over, over, over
Yes, the day was over...

Ivan Newby (8)
Avenue Junior School, Norwich

Flump

Flump
Gizzle wizzer, baby muncher,
Toddler cruncher.

One lonely night,
A lonely bear and his lonely owner
That owner threw him away.

Cute eyes like a night without stars
Bloodshot teeth to munch and crunch
Torn, scarred, black skin
Teleporter, shape-shifter
Will you be free?

Gregor Rogers (9)
Avenue Junior School, Norwich

The Indestructible Monster

In a miniature, enchanting, slimy forest
There was a snake-like, spotty, flying, mechanical monster
With eyes as bright as the sun itself
It left for the city and started to destroy it
Next, it left for the city hall in town
And when that was destroyed,
It went back to the forest and never came back again.

Giorgio Mckenzie (8)
Avenue Junior School, Norwich

Cutey Book

Botto is fluffy, short and clever
He can fly because his tail
Is separated like a helicopter
He has got orange, big eyes
He has three friends,
One is a cat with six eyes.
His other friend is a dog with six legs
And he has got one eye
And his last friend is
An elephant with five eyes.

Felicity Colyer-O'Brien (7)
Avenue Junior School, Norwich

My Monster

My monster is fluffy
Her name is Scary
She has a cute baby
She lives in a jungle far away
They like going to space where aliens live
The place they live is black and red
They go to a play area one day
They sleep on a beautiful bed
In a stranger's house in the jungle.

Florence Josephine Mae Warner (7)
Avenue Junior School, Norwich

My Friend Monster

I have a friend, her name is Bongily Boo
She is fluffy, she has a unicorn horn
Sticking out of her head
She chats a lot, she is nice
She has ruby-red eyes
We love going on adventures
My favourite country is Norway
She has got a little baby sister
Her name is Boo Boo.

Aksharaa Subashkaran (7)
Avenue Junior School, Norwich

Scramy, He Looks Like A Biscuit!

Scramy came from the River Thames
He is shaped like a biscuit
He's as cuddly as a kitten and one day,
He came out of the River Thames
And the people were scared of him
So the police came and put him in jail
So I broke him out and he gave me a biscuit and went home.

Jacob Willgress-Quinn (8)
Avenue Junior School, Norwich

Coconut

I met Coconut on a skyscraper in New York
He followed me everywhere in New York
And when I was on my way back to England
He flew when I looked out of the window
When I was older, I was an inventor
Inventing flying cars with no wings
And we had a turn on it every day.

Alex Wilson (8)
Avenue Junior School, Norwich

Mickey The Funny And Naughty Monster

It has clear, glowing eyes
It has yellow antennae that smell like bananas
I saw Mickey making mischief so
I put a spell on him
I turned him into a mouse randomly
He appeared in Dishland and found a naughty monster
That turned into a mouse
That was named Minnie.

Lily Mae Blunsten (8)
Avenue Junior School, Norwich

The Four-Horned Gentle Monster

M onsters are naughty but sometimes they're good
O ne monster who is very good and clever
N ice monster.
S o sometimes, they are naughty
T oo cute and fluffy
E ven now he dribbles and slurps
R eally, don't go near...

Jemima Kirkham (9)
Avenue Junior School, Norwich

The Monster

The monster came from Deadly City
He is bad and small and made for spying
It's red and black with metal skin
And symmetrical and deadly
And hot to touch
He is very naughty
And scares people out of their houses
That's why he doesn't have friends.

William Shaw (8)
Avenue Junior School, Norwich

Fluffy Monster

My monster is called Fluffy
She is green, soft and cuddly
She is short and has four friends
One is called Grace
And she is Fluffy's best friend
She is very good
She likes bogs and exploring
She comes from the woods
She is as soft as a teddy.

Angel (8)
Avenue Junior School, Norwich

The Octoperus

It was a normal day
Walking by a cliff
And then... I got pushed off
Arghhhhh!
I luckily landed in water
But then I saw... something
It was as big as a Viking ship
It looked like an octopus
And then it vanished
That night, I felt my fright.

Nikolai Brookes (9)
Avenue Junior School, Norwich

Slimy Slabawoka

Slime-trailer
Antenna-eyes
Shrieking cries from its mouth
Teeth like daggers
Spotted fur
A killer
You may be hunted so watch out
You may be hunted so beware
Oh and by the way, don't dare...

Martha Selby (9)
Avenue Junior School, Norwich

The Slugglop

The Slugglop
Born in a dark cave
Its skin rough, slimy, bumpy, flaky
Red eyes like lava
Smells like fresh dog poo.

Its teeth, oh don't get me started
On its crooked, wobbly, brown teeth.

Luca Seatter-Jones (9)
Avenue Junior School, Norwich

Pinky

Pinky lives in Monster Village
She had colossal blue eyes
She was as fluffy as clouds in the sky
She went to London
She was as pink as cotton candy
Fangs as sharp as blades.

Chloe Fleming (8)
Avenue Junior School, Norwich

Bob The Beastly

Bob was as clever as the universe
Because he was born in school
You would say he was cute
I say he gobbled me up
His name was Bob the Beastly
His cleverness was evil.

Percy Manka-Taylor (8)
Avenue Junior School, Norwich

The Jungle Monster

It was born in the jungle
It was creepy
We went to the park
And then it ate me
But I had a knife and
I cut it open
And I ran home.

Dylann Bothma (8)
Avenue Junior School, Norwich

The Hairy Flimp

The Hairy Flimp dwells at night
Scares everything it finds
He lives on Mars
Eats anything in mind
Beware of the Hairy Flimp.

Ruby Hauxwell-Baldwin (9)
Avenue Junior School, Norwich

Hone Thing

Annoying-beast
Mini-warrior
Snake-slayer
Rock-houser
Small-scuttler
Mega-consumer
Arghhhh, they cry!

Jack Bailey (9)
Avenue Junior School, Norwich

Gob!

G oing to stop you
O n his way
B ow down to Gob!

Oscar Colyer-O'Brien (8)
Avenue Junior School, Norwich

Under The Bed

The monster under my bed,
Is loud, noisy and ear-piercing
And when I clamber onto my bed at night,
He'll scramble around, going *ding, ding!*

The monster under my bed,
Has two eyes at the front and back of his head
So when he catches me doing something wrong,
My cheeks burn up, going bright red!

The monster under my bed,
Is awfully silly and bad-behaving
He's rude when I tell him to go away
Which makes him go really raving!

The monster under my bed
Has smelly and stinky feet,
So when he takes his socks off to sleep,
Well, let's just say, it's the complete opposite to a treat!

The monster under my bed,
Is always extremely greedy

He steals from my emergency snacks draw,
And gobbles them up when he hears me coming!

The monster under my bed,
Is a slimy and brown colour,
So he can make himself camouflage outdoors,
And uses the advantage against me as a concealer!

The monster under my bed
Can be the master of mysteries
So when I come to my room after dinner,
I can't find him, so my day, for once, hasn't been full of miseries!

Éléna Inacio (10)
Cromer Junior School, Cromer

Unicorn The Hero Of All

My name is Unicorn, you might think I'm nice
But when you see my rattlesnake, tarantula, bat, demon, ghost look
And my fangs dripping with mice,
I bet you'd be like the townspeople shouting,
"Look, here he is!"
The adults and kids would run inside
But the dads protect the mums
Until the ninth of December, I met a girl called Luna,
"Follow me to the volcano top and the Earth will love you sooner."
I don't know why she said that but she told me she was a wolf
That liked to hop so this is what happened on that volcano top
She pushed me in the lava, I shouted, "Hey!"
A big comet of fire came flying this way
The town screamed, "Oh no! Oh no!"
I told the comet to stop it and that made it go!
Everybody shouted, "Thank you Unicorn, hooray! Hooray!"

Then Luna whispered in my ear, "This is your lucky day."
My name is Unicorn and I am nice
I've got over 150 friends but Luna said this today,
"You told them your name twice."
By the way, I am not a unicorn!

Ava Skillen (9)
Cromer Junior School, Cromer

The Dreams Twoggle Would Have

Twoggle dreamed big, thick
He often dreamed under a tree
He would dream of being the first
Scientist to make a smart machine,
The smart machine would do anything
In your house, even clean
He also dreamed about science and biology,
Even made up science words like findology,
But Twoggle also dreamed about Minvillage,
He dreamed of making chaotic potions
With a bit of a twist and an edge,
He'd dreamed that they'd go bang,
Fizzle, pop, all through the night
In the morning, he'd hide them
And when they went off
They gave monsters a fright,
But not just that...
Sometimes he'd dream of the little things
That made the monsters happy

He dreamed of himself helping out monsters,
Helping them through the day when things got tough,
Then all of a sudden, *poof!*
Twoggle woke up and thought,
Wow, what would happen if
I did those things for real, what would happen then?
So Twoggle dreamed and dreamed that afternoon,
So I have to say that he might do those things soon.

Molly Jayne Postle (10)
Cromer Junior School, Cromer

The Playground Ways

Running, skipping, caring, dancing all day long
Never stopping, hoping, dropping food every day, no delay, every way
Friendship break-ups, always happening
Never stopping, bogey-picking, fall and drop on the floor
Fall and slip so be careful
Teachers are sometimes harsh but they care for you and me
And break time is just instantly everyone starting to cry,
Shivering, moaning all the time, never stopping
Wrapper dropping, running to the loo
Ice cream van honks his horn, everyone has some money
And ice cream on the floor, drooling
Roaring for ice cream, more! Everybody shouts,
Screaming all day for some more until their little tummies are full
It's finally the end of the day so everybody go away
Shouts the headteacher, go to your tiny homes.

Daisy Goodwin (8) & Scarlett Keeler
Cromer Junior School, Cromer

Oh How Nice It Is To Be A Monster

"Oh, how nice it is to be a monster
So smelly, scary and mean,"
Whispered Smelly Booger Bottom
Getting ready to scare a child
But before the scary monster had a chance
The child said, "Mommy, is there something under my bed?"
So as the mother looked under the bed
To her horror, a monster was waiting
So she called for the dad to keep their child safe
Then she went to the store to
Buy some supplies to set up a trap
When she got home, she made the trap
Got the monster to follow her
And it fell into her trap
"Goodbye," he sulked as he faded away
When the light shone on the cage
"Hooray!" cried her son and the dad
As she hugged them tightly in her arms.

Leah Louise Dawson (10)
Cromer Junior School, Cromer

Monster Under My Bed

There once was a monster called Big Mouth
He lived under my bed,
Oh how much the bed made me dread
Every night, Big Mouth would sneak up
And pop into my dream
Then when I woke up
That morning he would be gone!

There once was a monster called Big Mouth
He lived under my bed,
Oh how much the bed made me dread
Every day the poor thing would just lay there
All lonely and poor
Oh, if only I could see him
Because I could be his friend, instead of yours!

There once was a monster called Big Mouth
He lived under my bed
I didn't know what to do with him
So I took him back home
To the Planet of Monsters
Like a good friend would do.

Hazel Broughton (9)
Cromer Junior School, Cromer

The Monster Machine

The Monster Machine was not very clean
It smelt like the rubbish dump
Rumbling and grumbling it did all day
Chewing a big clothes clump.

The Monster Machine was not very nice
It had no friends at all
T-shirts and trousers went round and round,
Dizzy and close to fall.

The Monster Machine was not very clever,
It didn't have much of a brain,
Moaning and groaning, it did a lot,
Emptying down the drain.

The Monster Machine felt very sick,
And didn't know what to pick,
Decision made, he said to himself,
"I'll stop being nasty and be a... *belch!*
Ah, much better, monster."

Ivy Broughton (11)
Cromer Junior School, Cromer

The Friendly Monster

Three-eyed Blobby was very sad
He had no friends and that made him mad.

Three-eyed Blobby sat on a bench
A monster came, her name was Drench
She was very wet and kind of fluffy
She heard poor Blobby getting all huffy.

Then Drench said, "Don't get all stressed,
I know life's hard," her soft voice said.

With a whimpering voice, Blobby said, "Okay, I'll try,
But I have no friends and I am very, very shy."

"I'll be your friend," she said with delight
So they played all day and they played all night.

Paige Matthews (9)
Cromer Junior School, Cromer

The Moon Rocks For The Collection

This is the little, dusty dwarf planet
That holds the moon rocks for the collection
This is the big orange monster
That guards the little, dusty dwarf planet
That holds the moon rocks for the collection.
This is the star that hunts the orange monster
That guards the little, dusty dwarf planet
That holds the moon rocks for the collection.
This is the girl who flew into space
And said, "Stop it or I'll put you in a bag."
To the star and, "Shooo!" to the orange monster
And stole the moon rocks for the collection.

Charlotte Daniels (8)
Cromer Junior School, Cromer

My Blue Monster

A monster came from under my bed,
All stinky and ugly and oh so blue,
He ran to my bed and ate all my shoes
Then back to my bed, he was tickling my toes,
I was so scared he might actually eat me!
He ran to my mum's room and sat on the bed
Ate all the socks and put pants on his head!
"I must go! I must run!" screamed Scales
"No! No! No!" I shouted so loud,
"Yes! Yes! Yes! My dinner is in five, I'm oh so slow!
I have to go, bye-bye!"

Summer Marie Mclean (9)
Cromer Junior School, Cromer

The Dream

Splodge was very strange,
I found him on a mountain range,
With two floating hands and peculiar pants,
Crawling on him were one or two ants,
Once I said hello,
And he was eating a marshmallow,
Splodge offered me one,
We had lots of fun,
Then I asked him home,
He gave me a garden gnome,
Suddenly, everything stopped,
I was in my bed
It must've been a dream,
But there he was, my best friend Splodge,
Next to me in slumber.

Matthew Aidan Williams (11)
Cromer Junior School, Cromer

Monsters

Monsters dribble, monsters drool
Monsters are mean, monsters are cruel
My monster ran away, I couldn't find him
should I say
And then I say, "Starlight, star bright,
I wish I might have the wish I wish tonight.
I wish I will find my monster in May tonight!"
At the park, my monster dug a hole
And put me in, his green fur turned blue
"I'm sorry," he said and pulled me out
We all lived happily ever after.

Darcy Dagless (8)
Cromer Junior School, Cromer

Blob And Spotty

Blob and Spotty,
Their hair is slighty knotty,
They come from a different planet
And fight the evil shape-shifter Janet.

They killed her on the spot,
They kill monsters a lot,
Her hair was red,
Now she is resting dead in her heavenly bed.

Now that Janet is dead,
They don't have to dread,
They can live happily ever after,
With a life full of laughter.

Issy Carey (11)
Cromer Junior School, Cromer

The Story Of Blob And Spotty

Spotty and Blob,
Have a really cool job
They fight evil creatures,
With interesting features!

They came from Picnic Planet,
To fight giant Janet,
They killed her in a flash
Now there's nothing left but ash!

Now Janet is dead
There is nothing for them to dread
They may retire,
And do as they desire!

Megan Hawkes (11)
Cromer Junior School, Cromer

Stimo Is Bad!

Stimo never does her best
She's always rude and she leaves a mess
Her life is short and she's bad at sport
Don't get near her, Stimo is quite mean
"Get away from me," she says, "because I can scream!"
What she's good at, so small but bad
Is... gobbling you up!

Ruby Giovannoni (8)
Cromer Junior School, Cromer

The Very Spotty Monsters

Spotty is very dotty
She's big and hairy,
She's also very scary
Her teeth are yellow
And she eats marshmallows
And she eats posts
That taste like a loaf.

Isla Gull (8)
Cromer Junior School, Cromer

Fluffy Amber

F luffy Amber is my pet
L ove Fluffy Amber I do
U nder the bed is her home
F ull of patience she is
F ull of love as well
Y ou would love her if you met her.

A nd she is a cheeky monster too
M y Fluffy Amber is a shape-shifter
B ut she likes her formal self
E xcited she always is
R eloved by me.

T hose lovely purple wings match her purple eyes
H er fluffy fur keeps me warm at night
E ver and ever I want her.

C olourful and bright
U nderstanding as well
T alkative she is but a good listener too
E xciting she can be
S ad she never is
T o be honest, I can't think of anything I love more than Fluffy Amber!

Rosalind Pope-Norton (10)
Eaton Primary School, Norwich

The Cosmic Dragon

From over the hills and far away,
The cosmic dragon came to play,
Looking for anyone
With which to share the fun.
There used to be a planet called Earth,
Happy, joyous, full of mirth,
But then one day, tensions rose,
It got too much and war did explode.
The cosmic dragon watched in tears,
As a kind planet with no fears,
Was torn apart by war and hate
When it could've had no such fate.
The cosmic dragon thought, *why?*
Why do countries have to spy?
Why do nations mistrust, making machines full of bloodlust?
The cosmic dragon flew away
Hoping that another day, another time, another place
The Earth was not to be fated this way.

But if we continue the way we do,
Where murder and violence is common in the news,
What will stop us too, from becoming a ravaged Earth?
Maybe... could you?

Natasha Simpkin (10)
Eaton Primary School, Norwich

Monsters

Do you believe in monsters?
If you don't, you should.

There are monsters taller than buildings
Monsters with razor-sharp claws
But then there are
Short, cute, cuddly ones as well
Different shapes and sizes
Ones with two arms but most with more
All with different personalities
But all of them with a roar.

They may look like they're about to eat you
But none of them would dare 'cause you're chewy, tasteless
And horrible
Some monsters with dark, fiery eyes, others with a sparkle in their eyes
These creatures are hard to find for they are way up high, good luck finding one!
My friend is a monster, a nice one
Fluffy and blue, he loves hugs as well, he is a good friend and you would love him!

You may be wondering how I know,
I know because I am a monster!

Bailey Philpot (10)
Eator Primary School, Norwich

Bouncy, Benign Bing

This person thinks I'm a tennis ball,
I'm being chucked around like one too,
My name is Bing,
I'm a kind, bouncy thing,
Whose favourite food is cucumber.

I'm a caring, curious creature,
With blue spots and glowing, yellow antennae,
I'm not enjoying
This horrible soaring,
Through the gloomy, dark sky tonight.

I can teleport really easily
From stars to planets to galaxies,
I am a species from Mars
My best friend is called Lars,
Who is a species called Flabbadoodle.

The cultivated creature critter,
With a long, sticky, red tongue,
Was put back into his shed,
With non-living things that have already fled,
And fell asleep on his comfy cushion of friends!

Isla Valpied (10)
Eaton Primary School, Norwich

Monsters Watch Out

M y monster's name is Ollie,
O llie is a cannonball
N estles up in a ball, whenever he is sad,
S o all of the monsters which are really, really bad,
T race his steps to find him,
E very eyeball you own will be plucked out,
R emember this monsters,
S am his best friend.

W ill murder you today,
A fter your death today,
T errific sights you will see,
C razy Sam,
H as laser beams.

O ut of his eye
U ntil you hear a snap,
T remendous murder tonight.

Ollie Williams (10)
Eaton Primary School, Norwich

Fangy And His Family

Meet my friend, Fangy
He lives on the planet Mars
With all his friends and family
Miles away in the stars.

He likes to go to Monster Merhille
The theme park of family fun
His favourite ride is the Wipeout
Which goes as high as the sun.

He sometimes is mischievous
Especially when it comes to food
So he sneaked off to buy an ice cream
Which tasted really good.

His sister is always moaning
And brags about herself
About winning the chocolate cake competition
Which is not good for her health.

Matthew Abbs (10)
Eaton Primary School, Norwich

Monsters Are Real!

Monsters really do exist, hard to believe I know,
You think they only come in dreams
But I've seen one for real, so...

Will you believe me
If I told you it had red scales
Or two long, twisted tails?

I know nothing like your bad monsters,
All furry and slimy,
Oh blimey,
Nothing like that, no.

Would you believe me
If I told you about its terrible fangs
Or all the bangs
Which will wake you up?

But if I said
He is right behind you
Would you believe me now?

Summer Geitner (9)
Eaton Primary School, Norwich

The Menace Monster

Many moons ago,
Deep underwater,
A horrifying creature awoke,
Ready for her slaughter.

Her name was Dotty Lotty,
She had not one friend,
So she lived in a gruesome cave
Why can't Earth ever end?

Suddenly, a volcano
It gave an ear-splitting grumble
Dotty Lotty scowled in anger,
As her cave started to crumble.

So don't go near Dotty Lotty,
She might come down your road,
She is very crazy,
What a silly old toad.

Isobella Lea Solomon (10)
Eaton Primary School, Norwich

Moy The Worry Monster

Moy the Monster sits at the end of the bed,
He takes all the worries out of my head,
His big googly eyes stare at me,
To make sure I'm okay,
Once Moy looked sad,
I knew there was something bad,
Moy said, "All the worries in my brain, won't go away again."
I knew what'd work, a big hug would get rid of this worry bug,
I held my breath and bam, all the worries had disappeared.

Florence Bacon (8)
Eaton Primary School, Norwich

All Black And White

The monster in this poem,
Is all black and white.

Those fangs, those fangs!

Eating up children between groans,
He crunches their bones.

And sucks the marrow from their toes.

Only one item on the menu here,
And it's not roast deer.

The monster in this poem,
Is all black and white.

But now the monstrosity has evaporated in the night.

Robert Alston (10)
Eaton Primary School, Norwich

Sylvester The Scary

S ylvester the Scary has no friends
Y et he really wants to be loved
L et him have a sweet or two, then he will agree with you
V ery careful you will be
E ven if you give him a sweetie
S till, he might be a meanie
T ake the time to know him
E ssentially, he's sweet
R ather than avoiding him, being together's a real treat.

Eva Whitehead (8)
Eaton Primary School, Norwich

The Monster Of Mars

We went to the movies and had some smoothies
He lives on Mars but he doesn't like chocolate bars,
He's big and furry but not that scary
I'm purple and short, I'm not afraid to fight
I only have one friend but I'm happy
I get lost in the woods but I found my way back to you
My favourite place is Venus but it's kinda scary
I live with my friend and my name is Jeff.

Olivia-Graice Overton (8)
Eaton Primary School, Norwich

Tomato Reaper

T omato is his name
O pposition is his life
M an is his gender
A ccuracy is spot-on
T eaming is his weakness
O pposition is his key.

R eaper is his nickname
E qual to his skills
A ssassinating wherever he goes
P ump shotgun is his gun
E liminating is his strength
R eaper is his nickname.

Dylan Vlotman (10)
Eaton Primary School, Norwich

Laserstien

L aser beams spilling from its eyes
A pair of bolts in its neck
S inging is its hobby
E dges to the door at minimum pace
R age is its feeling
S ingapore is where its species lives
T he edge of Singapore in fact!
I n a large mansion, it lives its dumb life
E chinoids fill its drawers
N ine hundred years in age.

Cole Bryce (8)
Eaton Primary School, Norwich

Dashicorn

D ainty like a ballerina
A s magical as a fairy
S hooting rainbows out of its eyes
H orns of magic power, not scary
I ridescent wings to fly in the sky
C urly tail of different colours
O range, red, yellow, pink and blue
R acing over shimmering clouds
N o one's seen it, have you?

Scarlet Mills (8)
Eaton Primary School, Norwich

Gillbert The Monster

G illbert is a cheeky monster
I have two friends
L issy is one of them and very kind
L eo is my other and cheeky like me
B ert is my dad but he is away
E aster is my mum and she loves cooking
R upert is my brother
T illy is Rupert's girlfriend but hates me.

Megan Flute (10)
Eaton Primary School, Norwich

Monster Types

M onsters are funny and cute
O bdob has a spacesuit
N otnots are a species of Mlop
S lubs like to belly flop
T icklopus just does his thing
E bdoibs are like a bee sting
R apbeasts stay up all night to sing.

Rudi Pearson Bray (10)
Eaton Primary School, Norwich

Googly-Eyed Monster

I'm a female monster with five googly eyes
I have two antennae and a mermaid tail
I live in the sea and like to surf against waves
I love being naughty, getting up to mischief
And exploring on new adventures.

Honey Myers (8)
Eaton Primary School, Norwich

Reaper

R eaper is his nickname
E qual to his guns
A ssassin is his job
P inpoint accuracy
E qual to the sound
R eaper is his nickname.

Guy Jackets (10)
Eaton Primary School, Norwich

Rainbow Monster

The rainbow monster
Born in a rainbow volcano
Has a colourful body and blue hair.
She is good and has sharp teeth
Rainbow loves going on an
Adventure to the beach.

Aamina Farooq (9)
Eaton Primary School, Norwich

Monster

Roman is scary
He's terrifying,
He's clever,
Very hairy,
Scary to everyone,
He hides in the day
And comes out at night.

Jack Christopher Grint (8)
Eaton Primary School, Norwich

Monster Poem

S cary monster, yeah, scary
C areful, the monster can bite you
A re the monsters afraid?
R azor-sharp, this monster has razor-sharp teeth
Y ucky monsters, eww yucky.

M oany Monster just moans
O h monsters are real or are they not?
N ails are very sharp
S cared monsters are sad
T earful this monster is scared so it is crying
E xcellent monster, no evil monster
R oar, where is that roar coming from?

Cyprian Dron (8)
Fairstead Community Primary & Nursery School, Fairstead

Rainbow Cat In The Rain!

R ainbows, rain, rain and more rain!
A nyone could get a cold
I n bed, nice and warm, do not forget your ted
N ow you better come out and play today!
B etter not get water in your shoes
O ops... Rainbow Cat!
W hat, did you get water in your shoes?

C an you change into some fresh clothes
A nd get some towels?
T o me, to you, you will be my friend.

Ruby Feder (8)
Fairstead Community Primary & Nursery School, Fairstead

1, 2, 3 Monster

The monster has no one to play with
One, two, three, the monster is roaring in the rain
My monster is scary and hairy
Four, five, six, she plays with the sticks
My monster is sweet and next minute,
She is stinky.
Seven, eight, nine, life is on the line
She is being much nicer sharing her toys
Ten, she is coming to get you again
My monster is scary and tidy.

Ruby Taylor-Moore (8)
Fairstead Community Primary & Nursery School, Fairstead

The Guy

This guy started out so lonely and got bullied every day!
He got told he was ugly.
So he told an adult and the bullies got told off
The bullies didn't like being told off so they bullied him more!
Once the bullies finished bullying, the guy got evil and got people afraid
As he got evil, he grew big and large and he wrecked the bullies for what they did!

Isabelle Akisanya (7)
Fairstead Community Primary & Nursery School, Fairstead

Slashwhap's Rampage

In an old mine, lives a strong, rampaging monster named Slashwhap
He's never releasing his spikes so that harm he does
He's rough and he's tough, he'll never stop fighting
He's always on a rampage, "Don't get me mad!"
"Only if you want to be hurt!"
He's furious alright!

Dylan Anthony Jack Mattinson (8)
Fairstead Community Primary & Nursery School, Fairstead

Hairy Monster!

My friend is not good so we go to bed!
Bet you cannot go to bed
And dream of a world of wonder
So be careful.
Mary Berry everyone, clap, clap
Everybody look under your bed
To see a monster under your bed
So be careful!
I say she will take you to bed
She's so gaga, that's what I say.

Isabella Higgins (8)
Fairstead Community Primary & Nursery School, Fairstead

The Smallest Monster

M outh is big
R are third eye
S ame as a friend.

T houghtful, fluffy monster
H elpful, flying monster
R ainbow colours
E arly riser
E ats apples.

E ver so clever
Y oung monster
E very day, she reads.

Miley Robertson (8)
Fairstead Community Primary & Nursery School, Fairstead

Monster Eater

M ost of the time, Googly is eating
O ld Googly went to McDonald's to eat
N ibbling Googly loved eating
S ubway monster, Googly loves eating Subway
T errible Googly, no food in town
E xcited Googly, ready to eat more
R ound and fat Googly, no food left.

Zarrel Dunn (8)
Fairstead Community Primary & Nursery School, Fairstead

Curly Fry

The Curly Fry was born in America
He has no friends because he lost them
He ran and when he looked behind him, they were gone!
Curly Fry has five weird eyes on his blue face
He has three big spots on his blue head
Curly Fry can fly with his invisible jetpack
While playing on his invisible phone.

Harvey Buonaiuto (8)
Fairstead Community Primary & Nursery School, Fairstead

Special Treats

My monster is feeling very happy today
Because he had some sweets
For his special treats
He is now so happy
So I ask him if wants to have some more sweets
He thinks there are too many special treats
Now he doesn't feel all that good
Because he chose too many special treats.

Laeila Buttifant (7)
Fairstead Community Primary & Nursery School, Fairstead

Gengar

G earing up for full moon thunder
E xploding everything on his way!
N uclear weapon, he is really nuclear!
G engar is unstoppable so unstoppable like nobody
A ngry forever he is and smashes everything
R oarrrr! Smash! Boom! Roarrrrr!

Antoni Ostasz (7)
Fairstead Community Primary & Nursery School, Fairstead

About My Monster

My monster is fluffy and his name is Scruffy
My monster is from Monster Land
His favourite place to go is the beach
His favourite colour is orange
He looks scary
He does not have any antennae because he isn't a grown up yet
He is really cute when he cries.

Kayleigh Buttifant (7)
Fairstead Community Primary & Nursery School, Fairstead

Curtis

C urtis is humble
U nusual, disgusting teeth
R uddy is Curtis' invisible dragon
T artle is not with Curtis
I 'm scared of them because they have sharp claws
S ure you're up for the fight? Because I would not be.

Curtis Grimes (8)
Fairstead Community Primary & Nursery School, Fairstead

A Monster Came To Earth

My monster friend is Charlie
He was born in Scary Land.

He came from a spaceship
He landed in my garden.

He had three antennae
He is purple on his face.

He is very slow
He loves picnics.

He likes slime cake.

Amelia Fysh (7)
Fairstead Community Primary & Nursery School, Fairstead

Googly Eyes Poem

G oogly is nice
O utside he plays
O utside he's joyful
G entleman
L ikes apples
Y ellow on him.

E yes are blue
Y eti kind
E njoying monster
S ensitive monster.

Kristers Trecaks (8)
Fairstead Community Primary & Nursery School, Fairstead

Eye Hungry

E vil
Y ou would be dead if you met him,
E ye is pure evil
C old-blooded he is
L obsters are breakfast for Eyeclops
O ctopuses are dinner
P uppies for dessert
S uper strong.

Zack Goncalves (8)
Fairstead Community Primary & Nursery School, Fairstead

Miss Monster

Miss Monster is hungry and all the time
She has to go to the bin
She saw her old friend so she ran up to her
Her friend remembered her
So she started to live with her
She wasn't poor, she was so happy.

Sofia Grisina (8)
Fairstead Community Primary & Nursery School, Fairstead

The Friendly Monster!

M onster is friendly
O h, are monsters real or not?
N anny loves him
S afe was the monster
T errified were the people
E xcited was the monster
R un away!

Aaron Gent (8)
Fairstead Community Primary & Nursery School, Fairstead

The Nice Monster

The nice monster is
Strong, powerful
Nice and fun
Good and giggly
Angry sometimes
And cheeky.
He's still strong, powerful
Nice and fun,
Good and giggly
And sometimes cheeky!

Jayden Shuttleworth-Green (8)
Fairstead Community Primary & Nursery School, Fairstead

The Sleepy Monster

S leepy in the night,
L azy in the day,
E yes that glow in the dark
E verlasting, unextinguishable, she never ever dies
P retty and good
Y ellow teeth that glow.

Daisy-Louise Xanthe Gibbs (8)
Fairstead Community Primary & Nursery School, Fairstead

The Tall Monster

The monster was as big as a very tall tower in New York
His arm was as big as the biggest tree ever in the UK
His leg was as big as Big Ben!
His belly was as big as a park
He was even bald, he was old.

Nikolas Kriukov (7)
Fairstead Community Primary & Nursery School, Fairstead

The Lonely Dragon That Died

Once, there lived a furious dragon
And his name was Machamp
With no friends, he played with his ball
To keep him happy
Then suddenly, a meteor crashed and
The dragon was no more.

Amaru Casaleiro (8)
Fairstead Community Primary & Nursery School, Fairstead

The Monster

No, no,
Please, please,
Do, do not, not
Hurt me, me
Because you, you are
Very, very scary
My, my,
Bots, bots,
Will, will,
Pick, pick,
Up, up you.

Ryley Michael George Bull (8)
Fairstead Community Primary & Nursery School, Fairstead

Florance

Florance came from
Monster Town.
Her four eyes
Are scary brown.
She's nice and fluffy.
Her teeth are
Rainbow-coloured.
She has beautiful
Orange hair.

Ella-Louise Audrey Lewis (8)
Fairstead Community Primary & Nursery School, Fairstead

Monster Land

M onster Linkalot
O utstanding monster
N aughty
S tand monster
T iny monster
E vil monster
R eal writing monster.

Darby-Cole Mannering (8)
Fairstead Community Primary & Nursery School, Fairstead

The Fluffy Poem

My monster is fluffy and deadly!
My monster has friends
My monster has antennae
My monster has blue eyes
My monster's the smallest
My monster is friendly.

Faith Good (7)
Fairstead Community Primary & Nursery School, Fairstead

My Monster Poem

Yes, my monster is scary
Yes, my monster is hairy
And yes, my monster is smelly
And yes, my monster is messy
And he is a bad monster
And has lots of friends.

Jack Bunting (8)
Fairstead Community Primary & Nursery School, Fairstead

The Sleepy Monster

S leepy monster
L azy monster
E asy monster
E vil monster
P retty monster
Y eti monster.

Jasmine Collison (7)
Fairstead Community Primary & Nursery School, Fairstead

Charlotte The Good Monster

My monster is a girl
And she loves to toil
My monster is happy
But very snappy
My monster looks scary
And is very hairy.

Mercedes Shackcloth (8)
Fairstead Community Primary & Nursery School, Fairstead

Epic Monster Poem

Giant monster,
Two eyes,
Super fluffy,
Pretty monster,
Shape-shifter
Stinky monster
Flying monster
Dragon.

Roberts Anisimovs (8)
Fairstead Community Primary & Nursery School, Fairstead

Ted

Shiny yellow
Colourful spikes
Red eyes
Big ears
Six legs
Red cheeks
Orange face.

Paris Curry (7)
Fairstead Community Primary & Nursery School, Fairstead

Naughty Monster

M y monster's name is Naughty
O h no, the monster has run away
N ever ever not a monster
S ometimes he will chase you
T he monster is naughty all the time
E very day, the monster hits people
R eady, here comes the monster.

Hayden Cork (11)
Fred Nicholson School, Dereham

The Scary Monster

M s Monster has vanished
O h no, my monster has caused trouble
N ever hit monsters
S ometimes, he will chase you
T he monster comes out at night
E very day he burns the school down
R eady, here comes the monster.

Charlie Steven Marchlewicz (9)
Fred Nicholson School, Dereham

Noah

M y monster is Noah
O h no, here he comes
N ever ever take his food away
S ometimes they get angry
T hey never ever take his food away
E very monster eats food
R eal monsters are scary.

Rylee Towell (11)
Fred Nicholson School, Dereham

Monster

M y monster is a lump of poo
O h no, he's covered in poo
N ever touch him
S ometimes he watches TV
T he end of the day
E normous monster
R idiculous.

Zak Robertson (11)
Fred Nicholson School, Dereham

Monster Fun

Me and my monster went out to play
Me and my monster went out to see what we could see
Me and my monster went out to eat yummy ice cream
Me and my monster went up to bed
To dream about what we did today.

Courtney Rebecca McDowell (13)
Fred Nicholson School, Dereham

Cartoon Monster

M y monster is called Cartoon Monster
O ne eye is blue
N aps in the day
S kittles are his favourite
T remendous
E xcellent
R ainbows everywhere.

Abbey Weir (11)
Fred Nicholson School, Dereham

Bert

M y monster is fluffy
O range spots
N ever nasty
S potty
T he monster has got a spaceship
E very day, he eats the moon
R odeo not her idea.

Jacob Christian-Luck (11)
Fred Nicholson School, Dereham

The Monster Man

M y monster is horrible
O h no
N ever nice
S limy
T he horrible monster
E nd of the world
R eally sluggy.

Maddison Malone (11)
Fred Nicholson School, Dereham

Mister Choochoo

M y monster is charming
O n and off
N ewer monster
S uper fun
T oo pretty
E ager
R eckless.

Kyle Ravanera (12)
Fred Nicholson School, Dereham

Angry Griffin!

Griffin guards gold and pounces on its prey
Beak yellow as gold and sharp as glass
Eyes glaring in the dark
Legs strong as metal
Wings powerful as lightning
Claws can tear leather apart
Feathers dark as midnight
Tail can break down buildings.

Bodhi Foulser (8)
Mundesley Junior School, Mundesley

Unicorn

Loving, mystical unicorn
Glistening, gleaming, sharp horn
White, pointy ears that can hear any sound
Eyes as dark as midnight
Back as smooth as a pearl
Magical, soft tail that swishes like a bunch of ribbons.

Ella Hamilton (8)
Mundesley Junior School, Mundesley

Emerald Occamy

Gleaming, bright eyes, the colour of amber
Mustard-coloured beak that glimmers in the sun
Indigo wings that shine like crystals
Long, shimmery tail, more beautiful than ever
Bright colours as sharp as thorns.

Mila Carlton-Paterson (8)
Mundesley Junior School, Mundesley

Griffin

A protective, magnificent griffin
A sharp, yellow beak, as pointy as a needle
Arrogant eyes like blocks of gold
Wings soaring in the sky
Fur as soft as blankets
Tail like a snake
Claws scratching.

Sophie Roberts (8)
Mundesley Junior School, Mundesley

Phoenix

Glamorous, majestic phoenix
Crystal-red eyes
Black, pointy beak
Smoky, burning, hot feathers
Wings like red-hot flames
Tail as soft as a pillow
Claws as sharp as a knife
Ready for adventure.

Isla Grace Thomson (8)
Mundesley Junior School, Mundesley

Fierce, Dangerous Griffin

Fierce, dangerous griffin eating its prey
Eyes as shimmery as the sun
Sharp, glistening beak like an axe
Feathers as soft as a puppy
Big brown body as heavy as a log.
Terrifying, deadly monster.

Sophie Ducker (8)
Mundesley Junior School, Mundesley

Pretty Phoenix

Brave, pretty phoenix
Beautiful black eyes
Yellow, pointed beak, as sharp as a pin
Crystal red feathers, as soft as cotton wool
Pointy yellow feet as sharp as teeth
Ready to fly.

Katelyn Freeman (8)
Mundesley Junior School, Mundesley

The Brave Phoenix

Brave, healing phoenix
Crystal red, pointy beak
Eyes glowing like intense flames
Feathers like black smoke
Wings the colour of burning hot fire
Yellow, wrinkly feet!

Sophie May Howard (8)
Mundesley Junior School, Mundesley

Fire Phoenix

Eyes are black as coal
A beak more golden than the sun
Feathers like fire, as hot as lava
Wings as red as cherries
A tail as long as a rope
Wings flap frantically.

Courtney Wymer (7)
Mundesley Junior School, Mundesley

Unicorn

Eyes glowing white and golden
Ears pointy, white soft ears
Horn pretty and wise
Swishing tail, purple and pink
Unicorn is magical to help and care for little ones.

Ruby Marsden (7)
Mundesley Junior School, Mundesley

Unicorn

Majestic, mystical unicorn
Beautiful, glistening horn
Pointy golden ears
Body as soft as a teddy bear
Tail swishes in the wind
Trotting in the moonlight.

Evie-Mai West (8)
Mundesley Junior School, Mundesley

The Marshmallow Unicorn

Colourful, soft unicorn
Pretty, beautiful fur
Powerful, golden hooves
Glowing, white, sharp horn
Lovely, fluffy tail like marshmallows.

Kiera Light (8)
Mundesley Junior School, Mundesley

Basilisk

Dangerous, colossal basilisk
Head huge like boulders
Brutal, deadly teeth
Slippery, slithering tongue
Emerald-green, bumpy scales.

Luke Gray (7)
Mundesley Junior School, Mundesley

Dragon

Dragon, dangerous and evil!
Eyes like the sun
Teeth like swords
Skin like flaming hot fire
Tail as sharp as lion's claws.

Millie Rogers (8)
Mundesley Junior School, Mundesley

Griffin

Griffin ready to pounce
In the dark sky
Eyes like a dangerous, powerful eagle
Ears dark as midnight
Sharp, pointed claws.

Matthew Taylor (8)
Mundesley Junior School, Mundesley

Soft Unicorn

Majestic, sharp-horned unicorn
Glowing, white, fluffy fur
Powerful golden horn
Brilliant, beautiful
Pretty, soft tail.

Imi Whiting (7)
Mundesley Junior School, Mundesley

Griffin

Two angry, beady eyes
One sharp, pointy beak
Two spiky, long wings
Razor-sharp claws
Storming away with its treasure.

Logan Reid (8)
Mundesley Junior School, Mundesley

Colourful, Magical Unicorn

A beautiful, majestic horn
Big fluffy ears
Ginormous cute eyes
Furry, soft back
Long magical tail.

Iwan Thomas (8)
Mundesley Junior School, Mundesley

Kevin Goes Shooting

I met a monster yesterday
And guess how I came across it?
My mum treated me
So I got a monster egg.
I looked after it so well
Felt a scuffle on my leg
In the night.

It was a monster
In my bed!
It was orange and furry
With blue spots all over its head.

In the morning
I had to keep it out of sight
Because my mum would scream
For breakfast, the monster and I
Had strawberries as red as fire, with cream.

At midday, I thought of a name
I called it Kevin
It started to get sunny

I realised Kevin changed colour
To yellow and blue.

In the afternoon, I went clay shooting
I took him with me of course
I got one noisy shot
Then I realised Kevin had disappeared
I whispered, "Where's he gone?"
He was chased by a brutal, brown dog.

I followed after him,
But I couldn't see him anywhere
I heard a noise
It was laughter
They were playing together.

When I took Kevin home,
It start to rain hard
Kevin turned grey and grumpy
He got bored in the car
So he started to draw
On the window!

At home, it was dark
We went straight to bed
In the night, something was glowing
I realised it was Kevin.

In the morning
Kevin was gone!
I saw a note
It said,
'I am going home,
I will come back. Don't worry!
Love Kevin'.

Lilly Hickling (9)
Sandringham & West Newton CE Primary School, West Newton

Monster And The Queen

Once, this monster got a letter
About going for tea with the Queen,
This monster has a body
As blue as the sky
And an eye as big
As an orange.
The monster set off on the train
And was at the gates
The guard said, "Who are you?"
"I'm the Queen's guest for tea."
"So I will let you little thing in."
"Hello, you look strange," said the Queen.
"Teatime!" shouted the Queen,
"Well, tuck in."
The monster said, "I need the toilet."
So he went to get in his disguise
For he is actually a nasty thing
Who is going to steal the Crown Jewels,
But when he got near
The guard jumped on
him...

Pleasance Allen (8)
Sandringham & West Newton CE Primary School, West Newton

The Slimy Monster

One day,
I went to the store,
As I found the slime,
I discovered they had more.

I took some that were blue,
I opened it and saw,
Something that was changing colour,
To green as grass.

A large eye opened
And a gaping mouth appeared,
I realised what I bought
It was a monster, I thought.

Just then I saw a leaflet,
For the weirdest animal ever
It's a competition held on Friday night
I was going to enter.

To my surprise, it was Thursday
I had to get prepared tonight

It was something like getting
Prepared for a fight.

It was Friday, now to wait
For the final few hours
Of the day, I hope
I will win with my monster's character trait.

It was time
For us to shine,
In the moonlight,
Above the world's height.

I put him in a cage
For the competition to start
And all the others
Were a work of art.

We lost,
My monster turned
As blue as the sea
And started crying.

The judges were done
They thought he was plain

But when they saw the colour change
We won.

In the end
We saw
This long-lost family
For once and for all.

Oliver Herbert (9)
Sandringham & West Newton CE Primary School, West Newton

The Rainbow And The Boy

I found it in the beautiful sky
It was the brightest colour ever
It was so kind
It gave me a pot of gold
It had big black eyes
It didn't have legs
But it could still move fast
It asked me how old I was
I said how rude!
Do you want to go for a walk?
Let me get my go-kart
You look too fast for me
We saw my dad filling his hoppers
The colourful rainbow told me
It was getting sunny
It was time for him to go
I said bye-bye
And in a flash,
He was gone.

Elliot Wright (8)
Sandringham & West Newton CE Primary School, West Newton

My Monster

One day, a micro silver spaceship
Landed in my garden
I went out there
And said, "Pardon,
You can't park there, it's my garden."
But a tiny, fuzzy thing popped out
As fuzzy as a paintbrush
It had wide, blue eyes with a great big smile
And devil horns and tail
I cried, "Mummy, Mummy!
There's a monster in the garden!"
"Pardon?"
I said, "There's a monster in the garden."
"Can you show me the way to The Great British Bake Off?"
Asked the monster
"Of course we can."
In the first challenge, he made
Green goo with worms in it too
The judges tasted it
It's delicious, so nutritious

What are you going to do? It is delicious stew
Challenge two for you!
Cake time
Each contestant has to
Bake a cake
My monster zoomed off
And started to bake
He made a cake in
Seconds
His won
And we all went home.

Darcie Askew (8)
Sandringham & West Newton CE Primary School, West Newton

Fuzzel, My Pet Monster

One day, I went to school
And I found a tiny ball
It was extremely small
In fact, six centimetres tall.

I grabbed my lunch box
And I found a blueberry muffin
But when I looked, to my surprise,
It was as cute as a baby puffin.

I discovered when she was scared, she would shrink
The creature was blue, purple and pink
I took her home but couldn't sleep a wink
So I think and think and think.

The next day at school was awful
She wasn't well behaved
She made tons of mischief
I just sat on my chair and prayed.

After break, I came in
But it was as messy as a bin

The tables were toppled over
And the books had fallen off the shelves.

That very same day
We went for a walk
But suddenly out of nowhere
There came a spaceship.

It hovered over us
And sucked her up
I wonder if it's her family?
Maybe... or maybe not.

Clara Moreland (9)
Sandringham & West Newton CE Primary School, West Newton

Cupcake The Monster!

One day, I was looking under my bed
And I saw a little, long head
So I pulled it out
But I ran about
It was hyper, no doubt about that!

I made it stop
With a clock
Let's take you to the beach
But I saw a peach
And said, "Would you like it?"
She said, "A bit."

Wait, let's give you a name
So you're blue, pink and purple, maybe candy cane
Now, what do you like eating? Cupcakes!
Perfect, that's what I'll call you.

Right, now let's go to the beach
Here we are,
Let's make some sandcastles
So we dug a hole to get some sand
But there was a massive crab!

It told us to dig deeper
So we did and found a
Treasure chest
We opened it up
There was a lifetime's supply of
Sugar cookies and cupcakes
Cupcake shouted, "Cupakes!"
I didn't know what to tell Mum!

Chloe Southwell (9)
Sandringham & West Newton CE Primary School, West Newton

When The Monster Came To Earth

One day, the queen was sitting
In her chair and saw
A massive spaceship in
Front of her door
She wondered what
Was inside of it.

She saw smoke coming
From the door and saw
A big, red thing at the
Door, as red as a tomato
It had guns in its hands.

The police came in and they had guns too
The monster had missed every shot and
Then ran out of ammo
And couldn't find anymore.

He got so petrified,
He went back to the spaceship
Then noticed it

Didn't have any fuel so
The police had captured him.
They had just enough officers
To raise him into the cell
He went behind bars for life.

The bars were so thick that
If you flicked them, it would kill you!
Now the monster will
Never be seen again
(The queen wasn't harmed in the
Situation, she is fine.)

Kaden Underwood (8)
Sandringham & West Newton CE Primary School, West Newton

The Day I Met The Queen

One day, I was
Walking my dog
When I saw
A
Monster.
He was juggling
A football
At
The time.
He was a brown
And
White, spiky
Thing
"Oooh, you like
Football?"
I
Asked. The monster
Came
Home with
Me

But then I
Received
A
Letter
That
Said, 'You are
Invited
To sit with the
Queen
To watch a football game'.
I jumped, the monster
Jumped too
The Queen sent a private
Jet
We met outside
The Queen said, "Let's go in."
You're as spiky
As a porcupine
We watch it
My team won!

We went home
Together in a private
Jet
When we got home
The monster disappeared
Into space
He was once seen in
The sky.

Henry McLeish (8)
Sandringham & West Newton CE Primary School, West Newton

The Day He Meets My Friend

In the attic, something I heard,
As orange as a satsuma,
I introduced him to Mum and Dad,
He was quite a footballer.

We strolled to the park,
He was quite a silly billy,
"Hi there," shouted my mate,
"What's up?"

We trooped my mate home,
Then me and Monster,
Playing Fifa 18
The score was 10-10
He stayed home
Then he got offered for a team
And they won the FA Cup!
We all cheered, "Hooray!"
All of us had a disco...

Sienna Fellowes (9)
Sandringham & West Newton CE Primary School, West Newton

The Monster Tries To Kill The Queen

The monster came down to Earth
For then he can be king
So he went where the queen was
Until he found the queen
In bed, having her breakfast
One of her servants came in
And knocked on the queen's door
The queen said, "Come on in."
When the queen saw an orange,
Green and a rectangle of
Black with sharp
Points, white spikes
She screamed, the monster spied the
Glittery crown beside the queen
He ran speedily, tried it for
Himself, he pulled the queen and took
His new crown!

The next day, the monster became king
On that day, everyone bowed
For the new king of
England
The king monster was
Proud of himself
The monster got his moment to be
King for a very long time.

George Wood (8)
Sandringham & West Newton CE Primary School, West Newton

The Monster That Ate My School Books

When I was asleep
I heard a deafening crack!
What should I see?
A silver egg glimmering
In the moonlight
It had a ginormous
Crack in it
It was silver, worth
A lot of money
Then it started to hatch!
Suddenly, a rainbow thing
Popped out
It had eyes as black
As coal and the monster's claws
Were as sharp as knives
The monster was so gummy
So I thought it
Would like a fizzy
Haribo dummy

The next day, I named
Her Gummy
So I took her to school
I took her out of
My bag
The next minute
She started to eat
The books then she
Ate my teacher!
I decided to keep her
Because she was so cute
I set up a miniature bed
Next to my bed.

Evelyn Wright-Thompson (8)
Sandringham & West Newton CE Primary School, West Newton

The Adventure Of Mrs Fuzzywuzz!

One rainy day
A monster popped out of my bed
I knew my mum would hear me
But I screamed off my head.

The monster was as furry as a sheep
The strange thing was
Half its colour had gone
But it still looked cool!

It was half-rainbow
With colourful horns like ice cream cones
I knew it was from space
I called it Mrs Fuzzywuzz.

We got to lots of different places
To find her colour
And I stuck colourful things on Mrs Fuzzywuzz.
But they were all itchy and uncomfortable.

When we got home
Her colour flowed back
But... then I turned half invisible
Mrs Fuzzywuzz had taken my colour
And flown away to space
She was evil!

Ella Southwell (9)
Sandringham & West Newton CE Primary School, West Newton

The Day My Monster Goes To School

One day, I was plodding to school
I found a terrifying monster
At Edinburgh cottages
My monster has light blue
And dark blue skin with
Pointy ears on his head.
He has sharp, fierce teeth
And terrifying toes
His toes are as sharp
As shark's teeth
I took him into school
He climbed on the table
When I told him not to
But he did and then raps
My, oh my
Then tables collapse
The teacher told him off
He was very embarrassed
When everyone laughed at him

When it was time to go
Matt, my monster, ran as
Fast as he could
And I never got to see him again
Before I even got to know
His last name.

Caitlin Jayne Ward (8)
Sandringham & West Newton CE Primary School, West Newton

The Greedy Ice Cream

One day
I was lying in my bed
I heard something creepy
I looked under my bed
I saw a twinkle of
A dark blue eye
Shouted, "Mum!"
She did not answer
"Mum!"
Not a single word.

I looked under my bed again
I saw purple and yellow
Legs and arms
"Hello there,"

Do you want to come out
With me?
She had long, yellow, wavy hair
We set off to the park
She smelt like hairspray
We met with pleasure.

An ice cream van came round the bumpy corner
She got a strawberry ice cream
With sprinkles
And sat on the orange roundabout
I decided I was keeping her.

Daisy May (8)
Sandringham & West Newton CE Primary School, West Newton

Ice Cream Eats All The Ice Cream

I went to London on a
Magnificent train
And I saw a monster
Hanging upside down
Under the incredible
London Bridge,
The monster was
As fluffy as a
Stuffed animal and
As skinny
As a sheep
She came and
Nearly tripped me up
And sniffed me all
Over the place.
We went to the
Ice cream van but
She was very naughty!

She ate all the
Ice cream
We went to see Big Ben,
Buckingham Palace and went
Shopping in a big store.

I went home on
The London
Train and Ice
Cream went
To hang, back
Under the
London Bridge.

Elizabeth Wright (8)
Sandringham & West Newton CE Primary School, West Newton

Monster Goes To School

I was walking to school, collecting rocks,
On one was a monster!
It had a potato head and three arms
On the left
Four on the other
He was huge!
I took him to school and
He ate a child and the head teacher!
He ate too much
And exploded!

Elliott Harrod (8)
Sandringham & West Newton CE Primary School, West Newton

YOUNG WRITERS INFORMATION

We hope you have enjoyed reading this book – and that you will continue to in the coming years.

If you're a young writer who enjoys reading and creative writing, or the parent of an enthusiastic poet or story writer, do visit our website **www.youngwriters.co.uk**. Here you will find free competitions, workshops and games, as well as recommended reads, a poetry glossary and our blog.

If you would like to order further copies of this book, or any of our other titles, then please give us a call or visit **www.youngwriters.co.uk**.

Young Writers
Remus House
Coltsfoot Drive
Peterborough
PE2 9BF
(01733) 890066
info@youngwriters.co.uk